24240

DATE DUE		
NOV 14 2014		
JUN 27 2017		

PINKY and REX
and the
Double-Dad Weekend

PINKY and REX
and the
Double-Dad Weekend

by James Howe
illustrated by Melissa Sweet

Ready-to-Read
Aladdin Paperbacks

Visit us at www.abdopub.com

Spotlight, a division of ABDO Publishing Company, is a school and library distributor of high quality reinforced library bound editions.

Library bound edition © 2006

READY-TO-READ is a registered trademark of Simon & Schuster, Inc.
Also available in an Atheneum Books for Young Readers hardcover edition.

Library of Congress Cataloging-In-Publication Data

Howe, James. 1946-
Pinky and Rex and the double-dad weekend / by James Howe; illustrated by Melissa Sweet. —1st ed.
p. cm.
Summary: Pinky and Rex share a weekend with their fathers camping indoors due to rain.
[1. Father and child—Fiction. 2. Camping—Fiction.]
I. Sweet, Melissa, ill. II. Title.
PZ7.H83727Plg 1995
[E]—dc20   94-9384
ISBN 0-689-31871-5 (hc) 0-689-80835-6 (pbk) 1-59961-075-2 (Reinforced library bound edition)

All Spotlight books are reinforced library binding and manufactured in the United States of America.

24240

To Zoey, Adam and Sy—
my rainy weekend camping companions
—J.H.

To Heidi and Jon
—M.S.

Contents

Chapter 1
The
Weekend Adventure

Pinky and Rex were swinging side by side in Rex's backyard while their fathers packed the station wagon in front of Pinky's house. As they pumped higher and higher, they called out a list of the best things about the weekend adventure that was soon to begin.

"Hot dogs!" Pinky shouted.

"Toasted marshmallows!" Rex cried.

"Sleeping in a tent!"

"Hiking in the woods!"

"No little kids!"

Rex laughed. Her baby brother didn't get on her nerves the way Pinky's little sister Amanda did. In fact, she liked taking care of Matthew. Still, she had to admit it would be great not having either of them around for a whole weekend.

"Just us and our dads!" she cried as her head almost touched the ground and her feet almost touched the clouds. It was then that she noticed how dark the sky was getting.

"Do you think it's going to rain?" she asked.

"No way," said Pinky. "We won't let it!"

Just then, Amanda came running into the yard. She was wearing colorful new sneakers.

"Look what *I* got!" she said, stopping short of Pinky's outstretched legs.

"Nice," Pinky said.

"Yeah," said Rex, "those are cool sneakers all right."

"*You* don't have new sneakers,"

Amanda pointed out.

"True," said Pinky.

"Yep," Rex said, "all we've got are old sneakers."

Amanda couldn't think of anything else to say, so she picked up a rock and tossed it into a bush.

Ten minutes later, she thought of something. "Mom's taking *me* to the movies!" she cried as she watched her brother and his best friend strap themselves into their seat belts and look much too happy for her liking. Behind them, the station wagon was piled high with sleeping bags, cartons of food and cooking equipment, and a brand-new tent.

"I hope you like the movie," Pinky told his sister.

Amanda frowned. "I will," she answered. "It will be much more fun than a silly old camping trip. And don't blame me if worms crawl into your sleeping bags."

"Okay, we won't," Pinky said. He pulled the door shut as his father started the engine.

"At last!" Rex's dad shouted. "We're on our way to the Great Outdoors!"

Pinky and Rex cheered. Rex's father had been talking about the Great Outdoors ever since they'd begun planning this camping trip. He was as excited about going as the kids were, maybe even more so.

Pulling out of the driveway, the four campers waved goodbye to Rex's mom, who was trying to get Matthew to wave back, and to Pinky's mom, who was telling Amanda to stop it now. Amanda had her hands cupped around her mouth and was shouting something at the car.

"What's she saying?" Rex asked Pinky.

Pinky squinted his eyes, as if that would make it easier to understand his sister's words. Finally, he figured them out.

"She's saying it's going to rain," said Pinky.

"No way," Rex said. "We won't let it!"

Two blocks later, the first raindrops hit the windshield.

Chapter 2
In the Car

"On top of spaghetti, all covered
   with cheese,
I lost my poor meatball, when
   somebody sneezed!
It rolled off the table and onto the
   floor,
And then my poor meatball rolled
   out of the door."

"What'll we sing now?" Rex asked as the *fwap-fwap-fwapping* of the windshield wipers reminded everyone of the steady drizzle that had kept them company since they'd left home an hour earlier.

"How about 'Rain, rain, go away'?" Pinky's father suggested.

"Can't we camp out in the rain?" Pinky asked.

"The problem is setting the tent up," Rex's father explained. "But I'd say there's a good chance this rain will stop before we get to—"

There was a crash of thunder, followed by a downpour so heavy Pinky's father had to pull over to the side of the road.

"Then again, maybe not," said Rex's dad, reaching into the glove

compartment and taking out a book.

"What's that?" Rex asked.

Her father showed them the cover, *101 Things to Do with Your Kids.* "Let's hope at least a few of them are indoors," he said.

Pinky and Rex looked at each other and broke into song.

"Rain, rain, go away.

Come again another day."

Chapter 3
The Great Indoors

"Well, it may not be the Great Outdoors," Rex's father said with a laugh, "but this is just about the greatest indoors I've ever seen."

"I'll say," said Pinky. "It's cool in here."

"It isn't just cool," Rex said, "it's *cold*."

Rex zipped up her sweatshirt jacket and followed the long line of people deeper into the cave. She had never been inside any kind of cave before. She hadn't imagined they could be so big.

"We're now one hundred and fifty-six feet underground," she heard the tour guide say. "The temperature is a constant fifty-two degrees. But it feels even colder than that because it's so damp."

"Not as damp as it is outside," Rex's father muttered.

Rex looked up at him. "This isn't the camping trip you had in mind, huh, Dad?" she asked.

Her father shrugged. "That's okay. I've always wanted to visit this cavern. So what if it took us a hundred miles out of our way? Wow, look at that stalactite. Or is it a stalagmite? I always get those two mixed up."

Pinky and Rex chanted in unison: "Stalagmite pushes up with all its might. Stalactite hangs down, holding tight."

When her father looked surprised, Rex added, "School."

"Ah," he said.

As they rode the elevator up at the end of the tour, Pinky and Rex agreed that there were two best parts about the cavern and one big disappointment.

"I liked the boat ride," Pinky said.

"And I liked when they turned out the lights," said Rex. "It was *soooo* dark. And it was really funny when your dad went *'Ya-ha-ha!'* like a witch or something."

"Or something," said a woman standing next to them. Pinky's father started to make a joke but stopped when her look told him she hadn't been amused. He smiled weakly and breathed a sigh of relief when the elevator door opened.

"I just wish we could have seen some bats," said Rex, stepping out.

"Me, too," Pinky said.

"There are some bats," Pinky's father pointed out.

They all looked in the direction of the gift shop. Life-size rubber bats hung in clusters over the cash register.

Rex's father smiled. "Just what the doctor ordered," he said, leading the way to the gift shop. "Rubber bats to chase away the rainy day blues."

Chapter 4

Camping without Bugs

Several hours later, Pinky and Rex bounced back and forth on the only two beds in the only motel room their fathers had been able to find. They pretended the space between the beds was a moat filled with open-mouthed alligators and sharp-toothed piranha. It would have been more fun with Amanda there to shriek each time one of them almost fell, but still it helped to pass the time while their fathers unloaded the car.

"Not a very big room, is it?" Pinky's father said as he swung open the door, his arms piled with suitcases and backpacks. He was dripping wet from the rain. A puddle quickly formed around his feet.

Rex's father appeared behind him. His foot puddle merged with Pinky's father's to become a small lake.

"I have good news and bad news," Rex's dad announced. "The bad news is that this is the largest room they have—actually, this is the *only* room they have. The restaurant closed five minutes ago, the rain is going to continue through tomorrow, and my left hiking shoe has a hole in it."

"What's the good news?" Pinky asked.

Rex's father looked at him blankly. "I don't remember." He dropped into a chair with a heavy sigh. Rex put her arm around his shoulder.

Suddenly, Pinky had an idea. "Can we move the furniture?" he asked.

His father pushed one of the beds away from the wall. It creaked but budged easily. "Why do you want to move the furniture?" he asked.

Pinky whispered in his father's ear.

"Great idea," his father said. Turning to Rex's father, he said, "Sam, we passed a fast-food place about two blocks before we came to the motel. Why don't you go pick up some hamburgers—"

"And hot dogs," Rex chimed in.

"Why don't we just go there and eat?" Rex's father asked.

Pinky and his father looked at each other. Sam eyed them suspiciously. "What're you up to?" he asked.

"Oh, nothing," said Pinky's father.

"Okay, okay, but if you're thinking of short-sheeting me . . ."

Pinky's father gave him a gentle
shove out the door and then quickly
got Pinky and Rex to help him put
Pinky's plan in action.

When Rex's father returned twenty
minutes later, he couldn't believe his

eyes. There in the middle of the
room stood the brand-new tent, with
four sleeping bags laid out in a neat
row inside.

"Wow!" was all he could say.

"Pretty cool, huh, Dad?" said Rex.
"We can't camp out, so we're
camping *in*!"

"And the best part," her father said with a growing smile, "is that we don't have to worry about bugs."

Pinky and Rex glanced at each other and tried to keep from laughing. There were four rubber bats waiting for Rex's father in his sleeping bag.

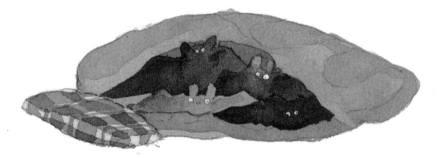

Chapter 5
Four Choices

"Best night's sleep I've had in a long time," Rex's dad said the next morning at breakfast.

"That's because you ended up sleeping on a bed," Rex said.

Her father smiled sheepishly. "Jake and I thought you two might like to have the tent to yourselves. Right, Jake?"

Pinky's father took a sip of his tea and, without looking up from the map he was studying, said, "Right, Sam."

"Sure, Dad," said Pinky.

"Uh-huh," said Rex. "It wouldn't have anything to do with you guys being *old*, would it?"

"Old? Us?" Rex's father scowled, but he was smiling behind his eyes.

"The way I see it," Pinky's father said then, "we have four choices of indoor activities on the way home. There's a reptile museum not far from here."

"Neat," said Rex. Pinky wrinkled his nose.

"Then a little bit out of the way there's a puppet maker's studio that's open to the public."

"Great!" Pinky exclaimed. "That's what *I* want to do."

"Only if we go to the reptile museum first," Rex said, sounding— to Pinky's surprise—a lot like Amanda.

"Then there's a train museum with an old locomotive that will take us for a half-hour ride."

"That's for me," Rex's father said. "I love trains."

"Finally," Pinky's father went on, "there's *my* number-one choice, an indoor miniature golf course." He looked up at three blank faces. "Miniature golf is *fun*," he said. "Besides, it's about the only sport I'm good at."

"Well, we can play miniature golf as long as we go to that puppet-making place, too," said Pinky.

"Wait a minute," Rex said. "I want to go to the reptile museum."

"Reptiles are creepy."

"Puppets are boring."

"Hold on, you two," Rex's father said as the waitress brought them their check. "How about we flip a coin?"

The waitress shook her head. "Bad idea," she remarked.

Everyone looked up. "Do you have a better one?" Pinky's father asked.

The waitress shrugged her shoulders. "It's only eight-thirty in the morning and all of those places are pretty close to one another. Why not go to them all? May as well make the most of a miserable day, am I right?" She took the money from Rex's father and winked at the kids.

"If we're packed and out of here by nine . . ." Pinky's father began slowly.

"Let's do it!" Rex's dad said.

"All right!" Pinky shouted.

"Do you think they'll have any iguanas?" Rex asked excitedly.

"Do you think I'll be able to make a puppet myself?" Pinky wondered.

The waitress heard the commotion from the other side of the room and laughed. "Wait a minute, you've got change coming!" she called out.

"Keep it!" Rex's father called back. "You earned it!"

Chapter 6
The Very Best Part

"So if you like spaghetti all covered
   with cheese,
Hold on to your meatball whenever
   you sneeze.
Ah-chooo!"

   "Rain's finally stopped," Pinky's
father said as the song came to an end
and they spotted the sign welcoming
them back to their hometown.

"You know something?" said Rex's dad. "I'm not sure we would have had as much fun if the weather had been perfect and we *had* gone camping."

"You mean that?" Rex asked, surprised.

"Sure. Why, if we'd gone camping, I wouldn't have had the chance to play conductor on a sixty-year-old locomotive."

"And I wouldn't have won at miniature golf," said Pinky's dad.

"You were pretty good," said Pinky. "I liked how you bounced the ball off that windmill. It really went flying!"

"I, uh, I meant to do that," his father said. "Well, at least nobody was hurt. And you have to admit I made up for it on the fire-breathing dragon."

The others murmured their agreement.

"Thanks for the puppet you made me," Rex said, turning to Pinky.

"You're welcome," said Pinky. "I like the rubber iguana you got me, too. It's a perfect friend for my bat."

"Dad," Rex said. "Can we try to go camping another time?"

"If you guys want to."

"Yeah!" Pinky and Rex shouted.

"Only *next* time," Pinky said, "maybe we can put up our tent in the Great Outdoors instead of the Great Indoors."

Pulling into Pinky's driveway, they saw Amanda burst out of the house. "It rained the *whole* weekend!" she hollered instead of hello.

"We know that," said Pinky.

"Ha, ha, ha!" Amanda said.

"Here," Rex said, handing her a large shopping bag. "If it hadn't rained all weekend, we wouldn't have been able to get any of this stuff for you."

"For me?" Amanda said. "You got stuff for me? Wow, look at this rubber bat . . . and a puppet . . . and a train whistle."

She blew the whistle so loudly that Pinky's father winced. "That may have been our one mistake," he commented.

"One mistake for an entire weekend isn't bad," said Rex's father.

Pinky and Rex nodded and raced across the street to where their mothers were waiting to greet them.

Later, after both families had eaten dinner at Rex's house and day was turning softly, slowly to night, Pinky and Rex were swinging side by side in Rex's backyard. They called out a list of all the best things about the weekend adventure they'd just had. There were so many, it was hard to decide which was the very best. Then Rex shouted, "Just us and our dads!"

Pinky cried, "That's it!" And he joined her in chanting, "Just us and our dads! Just us and our dads!"

Inside the house, their fathers looked up from the camping supplies they were unpacking and smiled.

"Who knows?" Rex's father said. "Maybe we'll get lucky next time and have another rainy weekend."